This Little Tiger book
belongs to:

_____

_____

_____

For my good friend Joan — C F

For Jeff, for your love and encouragement — A E

LITTLE TIGER PRESS
1 The Coda Centre, 189 Munster Road, London SW6 6AW
www.littletiger.co.uk

First published in Great Britain 2007
This edition published 2015

Printed in China • LTP/1900/1375/1115

2 4 6 8 10 9 7 5 3

Follow That Bear
If You DARE!

Claire Freedman   Alison Edgson

LITTLE TIGER PRESS
London

Hare loved bears.
He liked big bears, little bears,
hairy bears and scary bears.
   "If only I could find a bear,"
said Hare. "If only I could
catch one! The hairier and
scarier the better!"

So Hare bought a book: *The
Best Book of Bear Hunting.*
He opened his book
and took a look.

STEP 1

BEAR HUNTING

A WARNING
(please read carefully)

WHEN going on a hunt, to find a bear, you need to take the utmost care.

It's best to take a friend along too – choose one that looks much fatter than you!

"Podgy Rabbit!" called Hare. "I need you for a Very Important Bear Hunt!"

"A Bear Hunt?" said Podgy Rabbit. "How do you hunt for bears?"

"It's all in my book," explained Hare. So he turned the page, and they took a look.

STEP 2

THINGS YOU WILL NEED

*T*O catch your bear,

take a fishing net,

some string — as long as

you can get —

	L	S	D
	20	0	0
	10	5	2
	0	2	4
	30	7	6

A TORCH to shine
deep inside his lair,
and watchful eyes ~

BEARS LURK EVERYWHERE!

"Are you sure you want to find a bear, Hare?" said Podgy Rabbit.

"Of course!" Hare said. "The hairier and scarier the better! Look, I've found a fishing net, a torch and a piece of string. What's next?"

They turned another page in Hare's book and took a look.

STEP 3

TRAILING YOUR BEAR

Now bears are not always easily found, so look out for pawprints on the ground.

Crouch down low but please beware –

THE BIGGER THE PAWPRINT, THE BIGGER THE BEAR!

"I don't think I like the sound of Bear Hunting," said Podgy Rabbit anxiously. "I hope we don't find any bear prints!"

"Over here!" called Hare excitedly. "I've found some!"

"Oh dear!" said Podgy Rabbit. "They must belong to a VERY hairy, scary bear. Now what?"

They turned another page of
Hare's book and took a look.

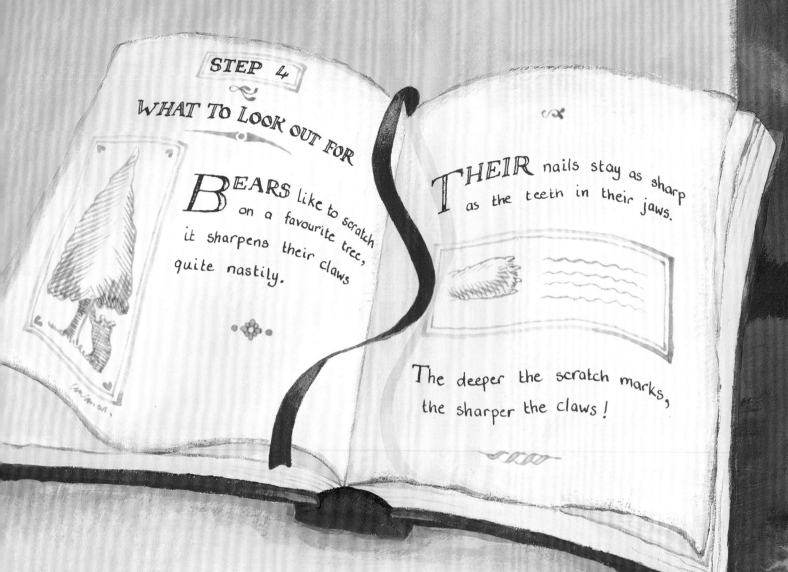

STEP 4

WHAT TO LOOK OUT FOR

BEARS like to scratch on a favourite tree, it sharpens their claws quite nastily.

THEIR nails stay as sharp as the teeth in their jaws.

The deeper the scratch marks, the sharper the claws!

"I really don't like the idea of Bear Hunting!" cried Podgy Rabbit. "Let's go back!"

"Not now!" cried Hare excitedly. "We're on the trail! And look what I've found!"

Podgy Rabbit looked. "Oh no!" he cried. "Now what do we do?"

"I'll tell you," said Hare. "It's all in my book."

So they turned another
page and took a look.

GETTING CLOSER AND CLOSER

WHEN a bear is close,
you may hear grumbling,
that is the sound
of his tummy rumbling.

HIDE yourself quickly
$H$and take great care—

the louder the rumble,
the hungrier the bear!

Rumble
Grumble!

"Shh! Did you hear that?" whispered
Hare excitedly. "That sounds like a
very hungry bear to me!"

"Hear it," trembled Podgy Rabbit.
"I was almost deafened by it! Quick,
Hare, let's take another look in
your book!"

STEP 6

MEETING YOUR BEAR

MEETING your bear can be quite shocking, don't let him see your knees are knocking.

SUCK in your tummy and try to look thinner, and hope that he's already eaten his dinner!

"Yikes!" gulped Podgy Rabbit. "Look over there, Hare!"
"Where?"
"It's a BEAR!"

"HELP! We'll never catch HIM with a fishing net and a piece of string!" trembled Podgy Rabbit.

"Just watch me try!" cried Hare.

"I'm HUNGRY!" growled the bear.

Then, suddenly . . .

"Dinner's ready," called Mummy Bear.
"It's bear-sized beans on bear-sized toast."
"Yummy!" said Little Bear. "Must go!"

"Come back!" called Hare.
Poor Podgy Rabbit was too weak to speak!
"Oh no," cried Hare. "I can't lose
my bear – that's not fair!"

Quickly he took another look in his book.

STEP 7

WHAT BEARS LIKE TO EAT

A HUNGRY bear with an appetite will eat up any food in sight.

And all bears hate baked beans on toast

But love ripe hares and rabbits the most!

Podgy Rabbit quickly grabbed Hare's paw.

"Run for it, Hare! It's lucky those bears have never read your book. For if they did, I bet they'd try to make a hare and rabbit pie!"